THE GOBLIN
IN THE GRASS
AND OTHER SCARY TALES

By Michael Dahl

Illustrated by
Xavier Bonet

raintree

a Capstone company — publishers for children

CONTENTS

Dear Reader,

When I was ten years old and writing scary stories, I had a special trick.

My bedroom was on the second floor of the house. My sisters' room opened directly onto mine. Their room had two unusual doors.

We did not like those doors. They led to dark attic spaces on either side of the house. We were sure something terrifying lurked behind them.

So this was my trick: I wrote at night with a torch, with my back to my sisters' bedroom. I thought that if I had my back to those doors – *and whatever lay inside!* – I would be scared. And if I was scared while I wrote, the fear might seep from my fingers and become part of my stories.

Like those stories I used to write, the stories in this book were also written when I was frightened.

Will you be **FRIGHTENED** as you read them?

Turn the page. Open the door...

Michael Dahl

SCARING
VINNY

"**V**inny! Stop scaring your little brother!"

"But he likes it!"

"No, I don't," said Vinny's little brother, Stevie.

Vinny laughed. "Yes, you do," he said. "You love being scared."

"I said stop it," Vinny's mother repeated.

Vinny rolled his eyes. "It's Halloween time," he said. "Everyone is supposed to scare each other. It's funny."

"It's not funny," Stevie said.

"You always laugh after I scare you," Vinny pointed out.

"I don't like that story about the ghosts under the bed," said Stevie quietly.

"They were gremlins," said Vinny. "Not ghosts."

"And no jumping out and shouting, 'Boo!'" said their mother. "No more fake spiders or rubber snakes. No more pointing out of the window and saying you saw a monster."

Vinny half-listened to her. "Whatever," he said.

His mother sighed and looked up at the living-room clock. "You two need to think about getting to bed."

Vinny rushed out of the living room first. He had a plan. He didn't care what his mother had said; scaring people was fun. Especially around Halloween time. And it didn't matter if Stevie screamed or cried, he always laughed about being scared when it was all over.

Vinny ran to Stevie's room. Something his little brother said had given him an idea. He would hide under the bed. Then, when it got quiet, Vinny would reach around with a claw-like hand and growl. It would be perfect!

Hmm. Should he growl like a werewolf or more like an ogre?

Vinny ran quickly to Stevie's bed and slipped underneath. He held his breath and waited. He heard footsteps coming down the hall. Then he heard the click of the light switch.

With the light on, Vinny could see that he was not alone under the bed. Next to him was a small collection of furry dust balls. Dust balls with eyes and tiny teeth. But they weren't actually dust balls. They were gremlins! They hopped up and down excitedly, without making a sound. The largest one, with a long tongue and spiky hair, jumped up on Vinny's shoulder. It hopped close to his face and then glowered into the boy's eyes, grinning.

"Let's all scare him together," whispered the gremlin. "Won't that be fun?"

THE NOT-SO-
EMPTY TENT

The Tropical Ranger Scouts from Tallahassee, Florida, were cleaning up a section of road on a hot, sticky July morning. They had only been working for an hour but already everyone was sick and tired of Avery Cooper.

"Don't step on that!" Avery shouted at his fellow scout, Henry. "That's a *Carnadina muscaria*!"

"Huh?" said Henry.

"A red-tooth mushroom," explained Avery. "They're very rare. Don't step on it as you're picking up rubbish."

Avery waved his hands at another scout. "Don't put your bag down there," he said. "Those furball ferns are delicate. They've only been blooming for a week."

"Got any ideas where I *should* put it?" asked Ben, the other scout.

Avery, hands on his hips, looked up and down the roadside ditch they were working in. "Terrible. This is just terrible," he said. "We are destroying this ecosystem."

"Which is why we're cleaning up the rubbish," said Henry, lobbing an empty drinks can into his plastic bag.

"No, no, we shouldn't even be here," said Avery. "We're damaging the grasses and plant life by walking around in our heavy boots."

Avery bent down, unlaced his boots, and then stepped out onto the grass in his socks. Carefully, he marched past the other scouts in their neon-orange safety vests to where their leader, Mr Marshall, stood in the hot sun, reading a map.

As soon as Mr Marshall saw Avery approach, he braced himself. *This boy is driving us all nuts,* he thought. He looked down and smiled. "Yes, Avery?"

Avery explained how their work cleaning up the ditch was actually making things worse. "We're trampling on all the plant life," Avery complained.

"Hey!" Ben shouted. "Look at this!"

All the other scouts were gathered around a flower in the shade of an elm tree. Avery pushed himself to the centre of the group. He looked at what Ben was pointing at and his jaw dropped and his eyes goggled. "A *Dionaea muscipula*," he whispered.

"It's a Venus flytrap," said Ben.

"That's what I said," snapped Avery. "Nobody touch it." He bent down to inspect the brilliant pink flower.

"Look at those teeth around the edge," said a scout.

"They're called cilia," said Avery. "Oh, perfect! A spider!"

A small white spider was climbing up the stem of the flytrap. All the boys held their breath as the creature stepped closer to the flower's gaudy, pink mouth. The spider clambered up the middle of the bloom, avoiding the long, tooth-like fibres on either side. But in less than five seconds, the jaws of the flower snapped shut, trapping the bug.

Avery straightened up. "See, Mr Marshall? This is exactly what I was talking about. The plant life here is too important for us to go marching around with our bags and our litter-picking sticks."

"Avery," said Mr Marshall calmly. "I have a special mission for you."

A few moments later, Avery and two other scouts, Roger and Dante, were stepping around bushes and small trees beyond the ditch. "Mr Marshall said that sometimes when people throw rubbish from their cars it lands all the way up here," explained Avery.

Roger leaned over to Dante. "He just wanted to get Avery out of the way," he whispered.

"So why punish *us*?" asked Dante.

In the first ten minutes, the three boys found drinks cans, straws, and crumpled up bags and containers from fast-food restaurants. As they walked deeper and deeper into the woods, farther away from the ditch and the road, they didn't find any more rubbish to clean up. The sun was high overhead, and the boys became hot, thirsty, and bored.

"Maybe we'll find another one of those Venus trap things," said Dante.

"I doubt it," said Avery from up ahead. "Those are very rare." Suddenly Avery froze. "Someone else is here."

The other boys walked up beside him. Avery was staring at a big khaki-coloured tent. It looked large enough to hold three or four campers, but there was no one inside. The flap was open, and they could see the clean, quiet interior.

"Who'd want to camp out here?" asked Roger.

Dante stepped up to the open flap. "Do you think someone just left it here?" he asked. "Maybe whoever owned it, like, died?"

Avery glanced around. "Well, there are no packs or sleeping bags. No rubbish, either." He sniffed the air. "But I can smell food," he said.

Dante sniffed. "Yeah!" he said. "It smells like chocolate." Cautiously, he stepped inside. "This tent is nicer than the one Mr Marshall has," he said.

"It is a nice tent," Avery agreed.

Roger joined Dante inside. "I bet a load of us could fit in here," he said. "And the floor is really soft."

The tent flap suddenly snapped shut. The walls of the tent swiftly collapsed on the two boys, trapping them inside.

"The walls are sticky!" shouted Roger. "I can't move!"

The walls folded in on themselves, wrapping tightly around the struggling Roger and Dante. From outside, Avery could see their human forms outlined in the khaki fabric as if they were covered in plastic wrap. Soon their bodies were wrapped so tightly they couldn't move their arms or heads. Then the tent began to shrink.

Avery watched in awe as the khaki-coloured mound grew smaller around its captives, dragging them down into the ground. Huge leaves reached out from under the tent and covered the struggling mass. After a few moments, there was no more movement and no sound, except for the buzzing of insects.

Avery hadn't moved the entire time. He didn't even notice the beads of sweat that ran down the sides of his face.

After what seemed like a hundred years, Avery whistled. Then, slowly, he said to himself, "That was the coolest thing ever." He turned and began walking back through the trees and shrubs. "An unknown species, I'll bet. Maybe I can even name it after me."

Avery kept his head down as he walked. *No,* he thought. *Maybe I'll just keep it a secret for now.* Soon, he could just make out the ditch beyond the trunks of the trees. He heard the voices of the other scouts. *Maybe I could show it to someone else,* he thought. *But I'll wait until tomorrow.* He looked up at the sky. *Noon. It should be hungry by then.*

WHY DAD DESTROYED THE SANDPIT

We used to have a sandpit in our yard, but we had to get rid of it. My dad destroyed it, actually.

My family only moved into town two weeks ago. We bought a huge old house, on the other side of the lake. It's a three-storey house, and my little sister and I each have our own room. I even have a separate room for my books and a TV for watching films.

The area is perfect for our two golden labs, Achilles and Hector. They have lots of room to run around. We have woods at the back, a little concrete building called a sauna, a blueberry bog, a couple of tyre swings, and we used to have a huge sandpit. I mean, huge. It could hold twenty people at once. Well, twenty children, I mean.

When we first moved in, the sandpit was empty. I thought the people who had lived here before us must have been really mean. They took the sand with them when they moved! My dad bought a dozen bags of sand and filled it up.

Unfortunately for me, my little sister, Linda, loved it. The sandpit sat behind a line of evergreen trees, and my mum couldn't see it from the house, so she worried that Linda might get lost or something. Every time Linda wanted to play in the sandpit, I had to babysit. I would take a book with me and sit on the low, wooden bench around the box.

After the first week, something odd happened with the sandpit. One morning, Linda and I trudged out there and suddenly she stopped and shouted, "Someone stole my sand!" The sandpit was empty.

When my dad came out to look, he stood there and rubbed his nose. "Where did it go?" he said.

"Burglars stole it!" cried Linda.

"Yeah, right," I said.

Dad knelt down, stared under the bench, and felt the sides of the box. "It must have leaked out."

"Sand burglars!" shouted Linda.

Dad said not to worry, he'd buy more sand and fill up the box.

Three days later, the sandpit was empty again. Dad nailed more boards to the floor and around the sides. He refilled it. And Linda went back to playing in it. She kept talking about treasures in the sand. Once she found a man's old-fashioned watch, and another time an old doll. I reckoned she just put them in there herself. We were always finding weird rubbish lying around the garden. For a while, everything seemed to be normal.

Then one day Aunt Dotty and Uncle Bob came by to visit. They brought my cousins, Mandy and Kyle. Kyle was my age so we usually played together. But my mum said the dreaded words: "Why don't you take Mandy out to see your sandpit?" What she was really saying was, "Robin, would you watch the little kids while they have fun? You don't mind being bored, do you?"

"Fine," I said. What else could I say?

We showed Kyle and Mandy the giant sandpit. "That thing is huge!" said Kyle. See, I told you.

Linda and Mandy jumped inside and started playing. Meanwhile, Kyle and I walked around. I showed him the rest of the garden, always keeping an eye on the sandpit. Kyle and I both like *Turok, Son of Stone* comic books. I had the newest one, so I told Kyle to wait with the little girls while I ran inside to grab it.

I had just picked up the comic from my bed when I heard the scream. I ran downstairs. Kyle was standing inside the doorway, panting, his face white. "Mandy," he stuttered. "Mandy…"

All of us ran outside to the sandpit. Linda was standing on the bench, crying and pointing. Inside the pit was a circular, cone-shaped dent in the sand. "Mandy's gone!" screamed Linda.

Aunt Dotty shouted and ran into the pit. Uncle Bob and Dad pulled her back. Then Dad carefully crawled into the remaining sand. He started digging through the sand, where Mandy had vanished. He dug deeper until he reached the wooden bottom. Some sand was sifting into the cracks between the boards.

"Get back!" yelled Dad. He hurried out of the sandpit. Then he and Uncle Bob grabbed one side of the box and lifted it. It must have been really heavy because they were both grunting and sweating. When the sandpit was removed, we all just stared. I couldn't believe it. There was nothing there. No hole, no tunnel – nothing. Just bare dirt.

Aunt Dotty knelt down and clawed at the dirt. "Mandy!" she screamed into the ground. Uncle Bob grabbed her shoulders and pulled her to her feet. Mum said, "Let's get the children inside and we'll call the fire brigade." We all turned to go, but then Aunt Dotty made a weird sound.

"That's Mandy's," she said, pointing. We looked at the sandpit in its new position, and saw a bright pink ribbon sitting on top of the sand.

"How did that get there?" asked Uncle Bob. Aunt Dotty stepped into the sandpit to retrieve the ribbon and suddenly, she sank down to her armpits. "Bob!" she shouted. "Help me!"

Uncle Bob ran towards her, but it was too late. She sank out of sight with a scream. We could hear her voice dying away as she fell. Uncle Bob and Dad lifted the sandpit a second time and searched, but there was no hole.

The fire brigade came and examined the ground around the sandpit. After a couple hours they told Uncle Bob they hadn't found anything. They told us that the whole town of Childers was built on sand. One of the firemen suggested they fell into some kind of sinkhole. But how could they sink through the sandpit with all the bottom boards still in place? And why couldn't we find a hole?

I guess Linda and I had just been lucky all this time.

Dad chopped up the sandpit with an axe. Then he built a fence between that area and the house. He didn't want the dogs running around over there. But a couple days later, I was calling the dogs and Hector didn't come back.

I know we've just moved into the house, but now Mum and Dad want to move. I don't want to leave until we've found Hector. I plan to go out every day after school and hunt for him. So if I don't show up at school one day, I might have sunk into the ground too. Or we might have moved. Just to let you know.

THE
FLOATING
FACE

Iris gripped the books tightly to her chest. Her long black hair swirled about her face. Her school uniform skirt flapped against her knees. She didn't remember the wind being this strong when she had walked to the library straight after school. But when the library closed for the night and Iris, the last one out, stepped onto the pavement, a gust of wind greeted her, a gust full of soot and grit that roared in her ears and made her shut her eyes. The rough breeze swept through the streets, ripping newspapers out of people's hands and knocking over rubbish bins.

Iris hadn't been watching the clock or paying attention to her phone. She had been busy skimming through books for her history essay that was due the next morning. And now she was late for dinner.

Iris got a better grip on her books and then set off for home.

A few streets away from the library, she waited for the lights at the pedestrian crossing. A pale piece of paper rolled and twirled down the street towards her. It never touched the road but danced and floated a foot above the ground. Iris was still waiting for the green light as the paper blew nearer.

There was no one else around. Not even any cars. Iris decided to walk across, and that's when she noticed the paper. It floated above the road and drifted towards her legs.

Iris expected it to be a square piece of paper, but instead it was round. Then Iris gasped. It was a paper face. A pale forehead, two curving eyebrows, slits for eyes, a sharp nose, parted lips, and a little white chin. *It must be a mask,* thought Iris. The paper face danced around her, caught in a whirlpool of air.

Iris walked across the street and the face followed. It never fell to the ground. It never touched her. Instead, it bobbled and glided around the girl. When Iris reached the other side and continued down the pavement, the face never left her side.

At one point she reached out to grab it, but the wind pushed it beyond her reach. Then she stood still and watched it circle around her.

Once more Iris reached out, but then she quickly drew her hand back. The floating face smiled at her. The thin pale mouth actually moved. And as she continued to watch, the mouth moved faster and faster in the moaning breeze. No longer smiling, it frowned, then grimaced. It opened wide, revealing a set of teeth.

Iris screamed and ran.

The paper-thin face floated behind her, never more than a few yards away.

"Somebody help!" called Iris. "Somebody!"

But she was alone. The streets were dark and empty. Only the wind and the wavering face kept her company.

Finally, Iris saw a teenage girl ahead, waiting at a bus stop.

"Help!" called Iris. "Please help me." The girl was turned away from Iris, watching for the bus. But when she heard the cries for help she turned. Then Iris screamed louder. The other girl had no face. Where her eyes and nose and mouth should have been was a pale white surface, smooth as an egg.

Iris watched as the face glided towards the girl, who bent down and reached out. The papery face, like a tame bird, gently came to rest in the girl's hand. Iris watched in disbelief.

The face, still in the girl's hands, moved its lips. "Thank you for finding it," it said to Iris. "I lost it in the wind."

The girl pushed the face onto her head, but now it was more horrible. The face had attached itself to the girl upside down. Her eyes were blinking on her chin, her mouth was near her hair. The girl laughed. "Oh dear," she said. "I'll just have to adjust it–" Then she stopped.

The upside-down eyes fixed Iris with a cold stare.

"No," said the girl. "I don't think so. I think – instead – I'd rather have *your* face. It's so pretty."

SPOT ON
THE CEILING

Mrs Lunder did not care for dogs of any kind. It didn't matter what breed or size or colour. It didn't matter if it was big, small, hairy, sleek, noisy, or quiet. A dog was a dog, and she would never let her son, Danny, bring one into the house.

"Please, please can I have a dog?" Danny asked for the thousandth time. It was evening, and he and his parents were sitting in what his mother called their "together" room. Mrs Lunder sat doing embroidery and Mr Lunder was playing a game on his phone while Danny read a comic book. Every few minutes he'd put the comic on his lap and ask, "But why? Why can't I have a dog? A puppy?"

"You know the answer," said Mr Lunder.

"Paul got a new puppy," said Danny. Paul was his friend who lived down the road. "She's really, really cute. Her name is Tulip."

Mrs Lunder squinted at her embroidery hoop. She stabbed it with a needle and pulled a long green thread through the fabric. "No dogs," she said. "Dogs drool."

"Tulip doesn't drool," said Danny.

"They leave hair everywhere," said his mother.

"We could get a hairless dog," said Danny.

She grunted. "Hairless dogs are the worst kind."

"Please?" begged Danny. "I'll take good care of her."

Mr Lunder chuckled. "The same way you took care of your pet turtle?"

Danny had stepped on his pet turtle months ago and crushed its shell. "It was an accident," he mumbled.

"The same way you took care of all those dead goldfish?" said Mrs Lunder. "Or the lovebird you let out of its cage?"

"You don't have a very good track record," said Mr Lunder.

"No dogs," repeated Mrs Lunder, ending the conversation.

That night in bed, Danny closed his eyes and thought of how Tulip had jumped up on his lap at Paul's house. He remembered how good the puppy smelled, how soft its black fur felt beneath his fingers.

Danny stared up at the ceiling, a frown on his face. His parents were being mean and selfish.

Danny noticed a spot on the ceiling. It must have been an old stain, but he'd never noticed it before. Maybe it was only because he was thinking so hard about Tulip, but the stain reminded him of a dog. A soft outline resembled a jumping puppy. A crack in the plaster lay where the puppy's mouth would have been.

Danny frowned deeper. *The only dog I'll ever have,* he thought. *A stain on the ceiling.* Then his frown softened. A smile touched his lips. *Well, it's something,* he told himself. *Better than nothing. Ha! I'll call him Spot. The perfect name.*

The boy fell asleep, dreaming of Spot crawling into his lap and licking his face.

Over the next few weeks, Danny would stare up at the stain on the ceiling every night and imagine all sorts of adventures for him and Spot. They would run together, they'd explore the woods on the other side of town, they'd visit Paul, and Tulip and Spot would become great friends. He and Paul could train them to catch balls in the garden or play Frisbee at the park.

Mr and Mrs Lunder did not notice that Danny had stopped asking for a dog. The subject never came up. And his parents never thought of bringing it up. Then one night, at dinner, Danny said, "Spot and I found a dead raccoon in the woods today."

"Dead raccoon?" squealed Mrs Lunder. She dropped her spoon into the soup.

"Who's Spot?" asked Mr Lunder.

"My dog," said Danny cheerfully, sipping his soup.

"You don't have a dog," Mrs Lunder said.

Danny shrugged. "Well, he's not like other dogs."

"Do you mean he's imaginary?" asked his father.

Danny nodded. "And he doesn't drool or leave hair anywhere or jump on the furniture."

Mrs Lunder wiped her mouth with a napkin, then folded it carefully on her lap. "I forbid it," she said.

"What?" asked her husband.

"We said no dogs," said Mrs Lunder. "And no dogs means no dogs."

"But–" Danny started.

"I don't care for any dogs in this house," said Mrs Lunder. "I have been crystal clear. And you went ahead and defied me by making up this … this unreal creature."

"It doesn't hurt anything," said Danny.

"I said no, and I meant it," said Mrs Lunder.

Mr Lunder cleared his throat. "Where is this dog, Danny?" he asked gently.

Danny kept his eyes on his plate. "In my room," he said. "Above my bed."

Mrs Lunder sputtered. "Above your–" She stood up and strode towards the boy's bedroom. Danny and his dad followed quickly.

"Where is it?" Mrs Lunder bellowed, pushing the door open. "Where?"

Danny pointed at the ceiling. His parents stared long and hard at the unusual stain. "Oh, it's like looking up at clouds," said Mr Lunder. "I can sort of see where you might–"

"This is ridiculous," said his mother. "A stain?"

Mr Lunder was about to speak when his wife cut him off. "This is going against my rule," she said. "This imaginary dog – this stain – is a sign of rebellion. Danny, you're being deliberately disrespectful." Mrs Lunder did not like being disobeyed. She stood silent for a moment, and then walked off, returning to the dinner table.

Danny gazed up at the stain. When his father quietly left the room, Danny turned and shouted down the hall, "I'm not being anything!" He slammed the bedroom door.

After dinner, Mr and Mrs Lunder went into their together room. Mrs Lunder stabbed at the embroidery fabric as if she were trying to kill a wild animal. Mr Lunder played his games, but he kept losing points.

"What was that?" asked Mrs Lunder. She and her husband looked up.

"I don't hear anything," said Mr Lunder.

A bark broke the silence.

"It's coming from Danny's room," said Mr Lunder.

The two grown-ups hurried down the hall back to their son's bedroom. Mr Lunder grabbed the knob and pushed the door open.

"Danny!" Mrs Lunder yelled.

The boy was not there. His bed sheets were rumpled as if he had been lying there only a moment before. His slippers lay on the floor. The window was closed and locked against the cold night air.

"Danny!" yelled his father. "Where are you?"

Another bark echoed through the room. It sounded further away. Mr Lunder threw open the window and stuck his head out. "Danny, are you there?" The bark sounded again, softer and more distant. But it was not coming from outside.

Mrs Lunder wept. Mr Lunder listened carefully to the bark and then looked up at the ceiling.

"Look!" he cried.

The stain was larger now. It had changed and grown. Now it looked as if the dog were running alongside its master – a small, smiling, and happy boy.

THE
FURNACE
MAN

Our house had an old coal furnace in the cellar. During the winter, Dad would march downstairs every night after dinner, open the furnace's big metal mouth, and shovel coal inside. Mum kept asking him to buy a new one, but Dad liked shovelling coal. He said it was good exercise and made him feel like our hardy ancestors who worked year round just to survive. He called them "stout-hearted."

"You better watch your own heart," Mum would say. "That coal's too heavy."

"Only one shovelful at a time," he'd say.

When the furnace made weird sounds at night, or the when the hot air began to sigh through the heat vents, it scared us children.

Dad said it was just the Old Man in the Furnace. The weird sounds were just the Old Man waking up, and the sighing was his laughter drifting up on the warm air. Dad thought his talk about the Old Man was funny. But it just made us more frightened.

When he went down to the cellar after dinner, Dad said he was going to go "wrestle with the Old Man." Mum rolled her eyes and told him to stop it. My brothers and I would stare at each other and worry. Was Dad really wrestling something down there in the dark? Was that why he was so sweaty and out of breath when he came back up? Or was it from all the shovelling?

A few times we went downstairs with him. He wanted to show us how the furnace worked, in case we had to do it ourselves if he was away from home.

Above the furnace door was a round glass window like a porthole on a ship. When Dad shovelled the coal inside, we could see the inside of the furnace get brighter and brighter. The light would change from dull red to orange to yellow. Once I saw some green and blue flames. "That's from copper mixed in with the coal,"

Dad explained. "The Old Man must be in a good mood."

One night, Dad took longer than usual in the cellar. Mum called down the steps, but he didn't answer. We all ran down and found Dad lying on the floor, the shovel in his hand. He was still breathing.

"It's his heart," said Mum. "Quick, call for help."

My older brothers ran back up the steps to call an ambulance. Mum and I stayed with Dad. She held his hand and bent her head over his chest. I could hear her quietly moaning. Then I heard another sound.

Tap … tap …

Something was knocking against the round glass window of the furnace. I walked over and looked inside. A man's face stared back at me. His skin was rough like coal, and he was grinning from ear to ear.

"Looks like I won," the man whispered. Mum screamed, and the furnace snapped on, the heat rushing through the house, the sound of laughter spreading through each room.

THE GOBLIN IN THE GRASS

Lisa stood at her bedroom window, watching moonlight turn the garden into a sea of silver. A movement in the centre of the lawn caught her attention. A creature covered in shaggy fur was crawling out of the ground.

Lisa didn't scream or yell for help. She didn't move. She stood there, watching. The creature's head turned quickly. It had caught her spying on it. The thing ran towards the house, and as it ran it grew tall enough for its face to be level with Lisa's.

It stared at her through the window. Its eyes poked out of its head on long fleshy stems. Lisa saw, close up, that the creature's shaggy fur was actually grass. Suddenly, the creature opened its jaws. The mouth was like a huge, hollow flower, with three separate tongues unfurling from its bloody red throat.

Lisa woke up with a start. It was morning, and sunlight was pouring into her bedroom. Her window was open, and she heard the sound of the lawnmower. She smelled the aroma of freshly cut grass. She quickly dressed and hurried outside.

Lisa lay on a deck chair on the patio. She hoped the sunshine and fresh air would help drive away the fear that lingered from the dream. She'd had nightmares before, but this one troubled her more than she wanted to admit.

As she lay there, soaking up the warm sunlight, she remembered a story her grandmother had told her. A story about a powerful creature that lived underground.

"The goblin in the grass," her grandmother called it.

The creature, made of grass and bark and flowers, lived within the earth. It shunned the humans, but it could grow dangerous and come above ground if it felt its home was threatened.

Lisa's father had finished mowing the lawn. Now he was spraying weed-killer. *Poison,* Lisa thought. *That's what weed-killer is. So what happens to the poison once the weeds are dead? Does it seep into the ground, deeper and deeper? Does it stay there forever, like a dark, oily underground lake?*

Lisa shook her head. She had dreamed about the grass goblin because somehow her grandmother's story had stuck in her brain. And because she'd smelled the grass through her open window.

Maybe some plants do get poisoned, she told herself. Maybe they grew twisted and ugly, or even deadly to the touch. But that didn't mean they would turn into a creature that could crawl up out of the grass.

Lisa walked into the house to have breakfast. Her mother was not in the kitchen as usual.

"Mum!" called Lisa.

Probably next door, thought Lisa. Her mother was proud of their garden. In the summer she loved to take her gorgeous flowers to friends and neighbours. Lisa grabbed some orange juice, then walked into the front hallway.

On a table next to the front door sat a huge vase overflowing with her mother's flowers. Lisa had to admit they were beautiful. Purple, green, and orange blossoms mingled with golden leaves and bright red ferns. Lisa didn't recognise any of the flowers, which was odd because she sometimes helped her mum in the garden.

Lisa felt a little light-headed. She could swear the flowers were moving. Several orange blossoms rose up from the middle of the vase. They rose higher and higher and slowly drooped forward, and then hung there like two neon eyeballs staring her in the face. The blood-red leaves were shifting back and forth. They fluttered in a sudden breeze. Lisa froze as she saw two hairy green arms burst out from the leaves and reach for her throat. Then she blacked out.

"Lisa … Lisa, dear…"

The girl slowly, painfully opened her eyes. It was too bright. Her mother and father were staring down at her. But where was she? This wasn't the front hallway.

"How are you feeling, dear?" her mother asked.

"Where am I?" Lisa mumbled.

"Don't worry. You're at the hospital," her dad said. "You're alright. You just fainted."

Lisa didn't understand. She shook her head.

"I found you in the hall," her dad said. "The doctor thinks there's a gas leak in the house. Someone's looking at it now."

"You'll be fine," her mother said. "You already look so much better than you did when – when we got here."

"A gas leak?" Lisa said.

Her mother nodded.

"It can be dangerous," said her dad. "That stuff is like poison. It can knock you out, or make you see things."

See things? thought Lisa. *Like plants moving, or green arms reaching out of flowerpots?*

Lisa took a deep breath. She did feel better. Afternoon sunlight gleamed on the metal frame of her hospital bed and the snow-white sheets.

"Can I go home?" she asked.

Her mother smiled. "Tomorrow," she said. "The doctors want you to stay overnight, so they can make sure it's all out of your system."

Her dad patted her arm. "We've been here for a while. I hope you don't mind if we run down to the cafeteria and get something to eat. We'll be straight back. Do you want anything?"

Lisa shook her head. She waved as they stepped out of the room.

The girl leaned back against the soft white pillow. She sighed. *What a weird day,* she thought. First the nightmare, then she'd fainted from a gas leak. She had been so silly earlier. Flowers don't attack people.

Her mum popped her head into the room. "By the way," she said. "I hope you like the flowers I brought from the garden. I thought they'd cheer you up. Be back soon."

Lisa turned and looked towards the other side of the room. A huge pot of brilliant blossoms stood next to the window. The window was closed, but Lisa saw the flowers sway in a breeze. They shifted back and forth. Back and forth.

ABOUT THE AUTHOR

Michael Dahl, the author of the Library of Doom and Troll Hunters series, is an expert on fear. He is afraid of heights (but he still flies). He is afraid of small, enclosed spaces (but his house is crammed with over 3,000 books). He is afraid of ghosts (but that same house is haunted). He hopes that by writing about fear, he will eventually be able to overcome his own. So far it is not working. But he is afraid to stop. He claims that, if he had to, he would travel to Mount Doom in order to toss in a dangerous piece of jewellery. Even though he is afraid of volcanoes. And jewellery.

ABOUT THE ILLUSTRATOR

Xavier Bonet is an illustrator and comic-book artist who lives in Barcelona. Experienced in 2D illustration, he has worked as an animator and a background artist for several different production companies. He aims to create works full of colour, texture, and sensation, using both traditional and digital tools. His work in children's literature is inspired by magic and fantasy as well as his passion for the art.

MICHAEL DAHL TELLS ALL

For as long as I can remember, I have wanted to live in a library. Or a museum. Or the Batcave. My current home has elements of all three, especially the library. I own close to three thousand books. A few books are more than a hundred years old. Many of the books are out of print. All of those pages, those voices and ideas, sit on my shelves night after night. And just as some plants silently spill their seeds onto the ground or into the air at night, I believe words and thoughts from those books seep and drift through my house in the dark. They plant the seeds of stories in my brain, where they wait to hatch and grow. Here are where a few of those seeds have come from...

SCARING VINNY

As a boy, I was nervous about alligators because I thought they could easily squeeze under my bed due to their shape. I was also afraid of marching bears hiding in the closet. Between the reptiles and the mammals (and the scary birds outside my bedroom window) it's a wonder I was able to sleep at all! And for this story, I wanted to make two twisty endings: One, where the imaginary monsters turned out to be real. Two, where the scare-er turns into the scare-ee.

THE NOT-SO-EMPTY TENT

I've always been fascinated by Venus flytraps. When I was five, our landlady, Mrs Johnson, had one sitting in the window of her upstairs apartment. I loved visiting her and would not leave until some poor, naïve fly landed on the hungry pink predator. What if there were a new species of flytrap, one that could camouflage itself from humans? And if it grew in forests, what better way to entice its victims than to look like something normal, like a tent.

WHY DAD DESTROYED THE SANDPIT

This story is actually based on a real event! My friend Aaron grew up in southern Minnesota, and when he was quite young his family moved to an old farm. There was a sandpit on the farm that Aaron and his sister played in, just like the one in the story.

The sand slowly leaked out of the real one, too. When his dad investigated, Aaron and his family discovered that the sandpit had been sitting over an abandoned well. They were lucky no one fell into the hole. I decided to make my story creepier by not having a hole underneath.

THE FLOATING FACE

In fifth grade at school, I read a collection of Japanese ghost stories. The one that scared me the most told of a man walking along a bridge at night, where he sees a young woman walking ahead of him. He politely says hello, but when she turns to reply, he sees that she has no face!

SPOT ON THE CEILING

It sounds weird, but I like staring at the ceiling. After a while, the ceiling seems to disappear, the same way it happens when you lie outside and gaze up into a pure, cloudless sky. There's nothing to see except blankness. Recently I was staring up at my bedroom ceiling, and instead of drifting away, a stain caught my attention. An odd shape. "How did I not notice that spot before?" I wondered. When I said the words out loud, the word "spot" sounded like a dog's name. Then the rest of the story began unrolling itself in my imagination.

THE FURNACE MAN

When I was nine, my family lived in a house with a huge old furnace in the cellar, its arms reaching along the ceiling and up into the first floor vents. It had an opening large enough for a child to crawl through. We children were always warned to stay away from it. Once my cousin Leslie stayed overnight and the unfamiliar sounds of the furnace groaning and sighing through the ducts scared her. She had a nightmare of a man, sighing and laughing, looking at her from the vent. Those memories have stuck with me. I often wonder, was that a nightmare or something more real?

THE GOBLIN IN THE GRASS

I confess that I use weed killer on the weeds that grow in my driveway. They push their way through the tiniest cracks to flowers with ugly blooms and jagged leaves. But this winter, while the driveway was covered with snow and ice, I've been thinking about the weed killer. All that poison. It says that it's not dangerous for pets or humans, but I'm not sure. I've begun worrying about it, like Lisa in the story. Maybe this spring, instead of spraying toxins at the weeds, I'll get down on my knees and pull them up by hand. I think I'd feel better. If there's something living under the driveway, or under my back garden, maybe it will feel better, too.

GLOSSARY

ancestors members of your family who lived long ago

cilia short, microscopic, hair-like structures

conversation act of talking with another person

defied refused to obey

delicate not very strong

disbelief refusal to believe something

ecosystem all the living things in a place and their relation to the environment

embroidery act of sewing a picture or design onto cloth

furnace large, enclosed metal chamber in which fuel is burned to produce heat

interior inside of something

rebellion struggle against the people in charge of something

sinkhole low area or hole in the ground that is often formed when soil and rock are removed by flowing water

DISCUSSION QUESTIONS

1. In "The Not-So-Empty Tent," Avery seems excited about a new discovery – even if it means his friends are in danger. What do you think happened when he returned to the tent the next day? Discuss the possibilities.

2. Do you think Lisa was really seeing a monster in the story "The Goblin in the Grass?" Or do you think it was her imagination? Discuss your answer using examples from the text.

3. Vinny is trying to scare his little brother, Stevie, in "Scaring Vinny." Have you ever tried to scare someone? Or has someone ever tried to scare you? Share your story of scaring someone or being scared.

WRITING PROMPTS

1. When Mandy disappears in the sandpit in "Why Dad Destroyed the Sandpit," we have no idea what happens to her! Imagine you're Mandy and write the scene where she gets sucked into the sand from her point of view.

2. The family in "The Furnace Man" hears laughter in their home whenever the furnace heats up. Have you ever heard a strange sound at night? Write a short essay about the sound and where you think it came from.

3. Sometimes it's good to laugh at the things that make us scared! Think of something you're afraid of, and try to write a funny poem about it.

MICHAEL DAHL'S

REALLY SCARY STORIES